This book belongs to

....

WIDE BIG WORLD

Maxine Beneba Clarke

Illustrated by
Isobel Knowles

LOTHIAN
Children's Books

On Tuesday at kinder,
under the mulberry tree,

Izzy Jones stared over at me.

'You're brown, Belle!' she said,
her eyes big-saucer-wide.

I said 'Yeah, I am!'
and I flashed her a smile.

Mr Jay said
'Izzy, I'm hairy
and tall.'

'**Your baby brother's**
cute,
chubby
and bald.'

'Belle's eyes are stormy-sea-green.'

'The sun's red-hot-brilliant.'

'The rain's cool and clean.'

Then I said 'Difference is everywhere, just look and see

'Izz, this whole-wide-big-world
is wondrous-unique.'

Mr Jay laughed.
'Nature's smart,
and wonderfully wild.'

'She sprinkles her sparkle

into every child.’

That day at kinder,
under the mulberry tree,
Izzy Jones smiled back at me.

'Clever Belle,' she said.
'Mama nature is wild

and the sun's burning-brilliant
and the world is big-wide.'

'And difference is everywhere: wondrous-unique.'

And we stood there, looking:
Izzy and me.

For Ayana and Jasmine
(MBC)
For Maureen
(IK)

Maxine Beneba Clarke is the award-winning author of *The Patchwork Bike*,
Foreign Soil, *The Hate Race* and *Carrying the World*. Poetry is her first love.

Isobel Knowles is an award-winning artist and animator. Her intricately
handcrafted work is colourful and playful. She has exhibited all over
the world from the UK to Switzerland, USA to Japan.

A Lothian Children's Book

Published in Australia and New Zealand
by Hachette Australia

Level 17, 207 Kent Street, Sydney NSW 2000
www.hachettechildrens.com.au

A catalogue record for this
book is available from the
National Library of Australia

ISBN 978 0 7344 1818 0

Illustration media: paper collage, digitally photographed
Designed by Jo Hunt
Colour reproduction by Splitting Image
Printed in China by Toppan Leefung Printing Limited